# We Wish You a Merry Christmas

### ❋ A TRADITIONAL CHRISTMAS CAROL ❋

First published in USA 1983 by Dial Books, a Division of E.P. Dutton, Inc.
First published in Great Britain 1983 by The Bodley Head Ltd
First published in Picture Lions 1985
by William Collins Sons & Co Ltd
8 Grafton Street, London W1X 3LA
Copyright © 1983 by Tracey Campbell Pearson
All rights reserved
Printed in Great Britain
by William Collins Sons & Co Ltd, Glasgow

# We Wish You a Merry Christmas

### ⋙ A TRADITIONAL CHRISTMAS CAROL ⋘

## *pictures by* TRACEY CAMPBELL PEARSON

FONTANA
PICTURE LIONS

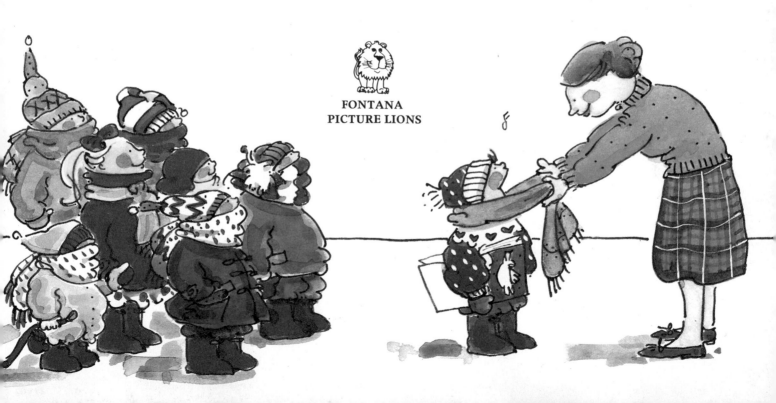

*For Mom, Dad, and Aunt Nini*

We wish you a merry Christmas,

We wish you a merry Christmas,

We wish you a merry Christmas,
And a happy New Year.

Good tidings we bring
To you and your kin.

We wish you a merry Christmas,
And a happy New Year.

Now bring us some figgy pudding,

Now bring us some figgy pudding,

Now bring us some figgy pudding,
And bring some out here.

For we all like figgy pudding,
For we all like figgy pudding,

For we all like figgy pudding,

So bring some out here.

And we won't go till we've got some,
And we won't go till we've got some,
And we won't go till we've got some,

So bring some…

out...here....

# We Wish You a Merry Christmas

Traditional Carol from the West Country of England

We wish you a mer-ry Christ-mas, We wish you a mer-ry Christ-mas, We wish you a mer-ry Christ-mas, And a hap-py New Year. Good ti-dings we bring To you and your kin. We wish you a mer-ry Christ-mas, And a hap-py New Year.

**2.**
Now bring us some figgy pudding,
Now bring us some figgy pudding,
Now bring us some figgy pudding,
And bring some out here.
Chorus

**3.**
For we all like figgy pudding,
For we all like figgy pudding,
For we all like figgy pudding,
So bring some out here.
Chorus

**4.**
And we won't go till we've got some,
And we won't go till we've got some,
And we won't go till we've got some,
So bring some out here.
Chorus